IN FAIRYLAND

The little Elves would cross over the border, and come into the King's fields and gardens.

IN FAIRYLAND

With the original illustrations by RICHARD DOYLE

and the text of THE PRINCESS NOBODY

by ANDREW LANG

Edited and with a foreword by CARY WILKINS

Derrydale Books NEW YORK

The illustrations have been reprinted from In Fairy Land:
A Series of Pictures from the Elf-World.
The text has been reprinted from The Princess Nobody: A Tale of Fairy Land.
Special material copyright © MCMLXXIX by Crown Publishers, Inc.
All rights reserved.
This edition is published by Derrydale Books,
a division of Crown Publishers, Inc.
a b c d e f g h
DERRYDALE 1979 EDITION
Designed by Ruth Kolbert Smerechniak
Manufactured in the United States of America

Library of Congress Cataloging in Publication Data

Lang, Andrew, 1844-1912.
In fairyland.

Text reprinted from the author's Princess Nobody,
published by Longmans, Green, London; ill.
reprinted from In fairy land,
by W. Allingham, published by Longmans, Green, London.
SUMMARY: The King and Queen
of the country next to Fairyland
long for a child
and are finally blessed with a daughter, the Princess Niente.
[1. Fairy tales]   I. Doyle, Richard, 1824-1893.
II. Wilkins, Cary.   III. Title.
PZ8.L15Im 1979   [Fic]   79-16656
ISBN 0-517-29353-6

FOREWORD

Having grown up in the Scottish border country—a haunted land of romance and legend—Andrew Lang was always attracted to the magical world of fantasy: a dream world where we can lose sight of our daily surroundings and enter a land of enchantment. He must have experienced this mystical feeling when he encountered *In Fairyland: A Series of Pictures from the Elf-World,* by Richard Doyle. Originally published in 1869 by Longmans, Green, and Company (London), it contained sixteen beautiful color plates (thirty-four drawings) and a poem by William Allingham. These exquisite, delicately drawn pictures of fairies and elves playing among the flowers with birds, insects, and other friendly creatures are considered by many to be Doyle's masterpiece.

In 1843 (at eighteen years of age), Doyle joined the staff of London's *Punch* magazine. Before he left in 1850, he had become one of its top cartoonists and designed the cover that became famous. People knew his magazine work by his monogram signature accompanied by a dicky, a small bird. Among the books he illustrated are Ruskin's *The King of the Golden River,* Dickens's *The Cricket on the Hearth,* Hughes's *Scouring of the White Horse, The Fairy Ring, Mr. Pips Hys Diary, The Story of Jack and the Giants,* and a version of "The Sleeping Beauty." Two posthumously published works of his youth, *Jack the Giant Killer* and *Dicky Doyle's Journal,* are delightfully amusing and display a surprising precocity.

Doyle's *In Fairyland* illustrations were reissued in 1884 in *The Princess Nobody: A Tale of Fairy Land,* by Andrew Lang. According to Lang's biographer, Roger L. Green, the book was probably suggested to Lang by Charles Longman, his friend and publisher. Because of Allingham's poem, which is of dubious quality and is only vaguely related to the pictures, *In Fairyland* was not really a children's book. Lang, a noted anthropologist who would later write several fairy tales and collect and edit tales for his famous series of fairy books, ingeniously wove a fairy tale around the pictures. He used several familiar fairy tale elements and wrote the story in a delightful, whimsical style.

Lang did not completely resolve the problem of keeping the characters recognizable throughout the story. For example, one has to stretch the imagination a little to see that the three couples in the pictures on pages 57–58 are actually the same couple in each picture. But, for the most part, Lang was successful.

Five of Doyle's pictures were omitted from *The Princess Nobody*, and many of the others were cut up and reproduced uncolored. Only a couple of the pictures were totally unrelated to the text.

In this edition, all of Doyle's illustrations have been reproduced in color. For those omitted from *The Princess Nobody*, captions have been created to relate them to the story. In addition, most of the other pictures have been given new captions and some pictures have been put in different positions so that they relate more directly to the story.

Lang's tale has been reprinted almost exactly as it was originally published. The main change has been to Americanize the English spellings. A couple of obvious errors have also been fixed: in one place, Princes were called Fairies, and in another, a passage that was repeated in a slightly different form has been deleted. And, in one of the pictures a winged insect appears, which Lang called a Daddy Long Legs. Since Americans use that name for a type of spider, we have called the creature a Dragonfly. One final minor point: Lang used two words to name his magical wonderland—Fairy Land. We have kept that spelling in the text but have adopted its modern spelling, as one word, for the title.

Here then, is the happily-ever-after tale of Prince Comical and Princess Nobody. As we journey from Fairyland to Mushroom Land to the Valley Magical, we rediscover the joys of "treading the ancient ways," the paths so clearly marked by artists such as Andrew Lang and Richard Doyle. They had the gift of recreating that forgotten world of long ago.

CARY WILKINS

LIST OF ILLUSTRATIONS

Feasting and fun among the fuchsias.

CHAPTER ONE

THE PRINCESS NOBODY

ONCE upon a time, when Fairies were much more common than they are now, there lived a King and a Queen. Their country was close to Fairy Land, and very often the little Elves would cross over the border, and come into the King's fields and gardens. The girl-fairies would swing out of the bells of the fuchsias, and loll on the leaves, and drink the little drops of dew that fell down the stems. Here you may see all the Fairies making themselves merry at a picnic on a fuchsia, and an ugly little Dwarf is climbing up the stalk.

Now the King and Queen of the country next to Fairy Land were very rich, and very fond of each other; but one thing made them unhappy. They had no child, neither boy nor girl, to sit on the Throne

Mischievous Elves and Fairies.

Dancing with a Butterfly.

(16)

Here's the King in mournful mood;
They'd amuse him if they could.

when they were dead and gone. Often the Queen said she wished she had a child, even if it were no bigger than her thumb; and she hoped the Fairies might hear her and help her. But they never took any notice. One day, when the King had been counting out his money all day (the day when the tributes were paid in), he grew very tired. He took off his crown, and went into his garden. Then he looked all round his kingdom, and said, "Ah! I would give it all for a BABY!"

No sooner had the King said this, than he heard a little squeaking voice near his foot: "You shall have a lovely Baby, if you will give me what I ask."

The King looked down, and there was the funniest little Dwarf that ever was seen. He had a high red cap like a flower. He had a big moustache, and a short beard that curled outwards. His cloak was red, like his cap, and his coat was green, and he rode on a green Frog. Many people would have been frightened, but the King was used to Fairies.

"You shall have a beautiful Baby, if you will give me what I ask," said the Dwarf again.

"I'll give you anything you like," said the King.

"Then promise to give me NIENTE," said the Dwarf.

"Certainly," said the King (who had not an idea what NIENTE meant). "How will you take it?"

(17)

"I will take *it*," said the Dwarf, "in my own way, on my own day."

With that he set spurs to his Frog, which cleared the garden path at one bound, and he was soon lost among the flowers.

Well, next day, a dreadful war broke out between the Ghosts and the Giants, and the King had to set forth and fight on the side of his friends the Giants.

A long, long time he was away; nearly a year. At last he came back to his own country, and he heard all the church bells ringing merrily. "What *can* be the matter?" said the King, and hurried to his Palace, where all the Courtiers rushed out and told him the Queen had got a BABY.

"Girl or a boy?" says the King.

"A Princess, your Majesty," says the Nurse, with a low curtsey, correcting him.

Well, you may fancy how glad the King was, though he would have *preferred* a boy.

"What have you called her?" he asked.

Here you see a Fairy host,
Fit to fight with Dwarf or Ghost.

(18)

"Till your Majesty's return, we thought it better not to christen the Princess," said the Nurse, "so we have called her by the Italian name for *Nothing*: NIENTE; the Princess Niente, your Majesty."

When the King heard *that*, and remembered that he had promised to give NIENTE to the Dwarf, he hid his face in his hands and groaned. Nobody knew what he meant, or why he was so sad, so he thought it best to keep it to himself. He went in and kissed the Queen, and comforted her, and looked at the BABY. Never was there a BABY so beautiful; she was like a Fairy's child, and so light, she could sit on a flower and not crush it. She had little wings on her back; and all the birds were fond of her. The peasants and common people (who said they "could not see why the *first* Royal baby should be called 'Ninety'") always spoke of her as the Princess Nobody. Only the Courtiers called her Niente. The Water Fairy was her Godmother, but (for a Fairy reason) they concealed her *real* name, and of course, she was not *christened* Niente. Here you may see her sitting teaching the little Birds to sing. They are all round her in a circle, each of them

All the Birds were fond of her.

She taught the little Birds to sing
Music fit to please a King.

singing his very best. Great fun she and all her little companions had with the Birds; here they are, riding on them, and tumbling off when the Bird kicks. And here, again, you may observe the baby Princess riding a Parrot, while one of her Maids of Honor teases an Owl. Never was there such a happy country; all Birds and Babies, playing together, singing, and as merry as the day was long.

Well, this joyful life went on till the Princess Niente was growing quite a big girl; she was nearly fourteen. Then, one day, came a tremendous knock at the Palace gates. Out rushed the Porter, and saw a little Dwarf, in a red cap, and a red cloak, riding a green Frog.

"Tell the King he is wanted," said the Dwarf.

The porter carried this rude message, and the King went trembling to the door.

"I have come to claim your promise; you give me NIENTE," said the Dwarf, in his froggy voice.

Great fun she and all her little companions had with the Birds.

Now the King had spoken long ago about his foolish promise, to the Queen of the Water Fairies, a very powerful person, and Godmother of his child.

"The Dwarf must be one of *my* people, if he rides a Frog," the

The Princess and her Maid of Honor.

Queen of the Water Fairies had said. "Just send him to *me*, if he is troublesome."

The King remembered this when he saw the Dwarf, so he put a bold face on it.

"That's you, is it?" said the King to the Dwarf. "Just you go to the Queen of the Water Fairies; she will have a word to say to you."

When the Dwarf heard that, it was *his* turn to tremble. He shook his little fist at the King; he half-drew his sword.

*The Dwarf and the Queen of the Water Fairies
have a long talk.*

"I'll have NIENTE yet," he said, and he set spurs to his Frog, and bounded off to see the Queen of the Water Fairies.

It was night by the time the Dwarf reached the stream where the Queen lived, among the long flags and rushes and reeds of the river.

Here you see him by the river; how tired his Frog looks! He is talking to the Water Fairy. Well, he and the Water Fairy had a long talk, and the end of it was that the Fairy found only one way of saving the Princess. She flew to the King and said, "I can only help you by making the Princess vanish clean away. I have a bird here on whose back she can fly away in safety. The Dwarf will not get her, but you will never see her again, unless a brave Prince can find her where she is hidden, and guarded by my Water Fairies."

She vanished clean away.

Then the poor mother and father cried dreadfully, but they saw there was no hope. It was better that the Princess should vanish away, than that she should be married to a horrid rude Dwarf, who rode on a Frog. So they sent for the Princess, and kissed her, and embraced her, and wept over her, and (gradually she faded out of their very arms, and vanished clean away) then she flew away on the bird's back.

The guest of honor at the christening of the Princess Niente was her Godmother, the Queen of the Water Fairies. Here she is arriving in magnificent style: perched in a light carriage, a twelve-in-hand, drawn by thoroughbred Butterflies.

After Princess Niente flew away from Fairy Land, everyone was in a bad humor.
Things just weren't the same without her, and everyone was sad and grouchy.

CHAPTER TWO

IN MUSHROOM LAND

NOW all the Kingdom next to Fairy Land was miserable, and all the people were murmuring, and the King and Queen were nearly melted in tears. They thought of all ways to recover their dear daughter, and at last the Queen hit on a plan.

"My dear," she said to the King, "let us offer to give our daughter for a wife, to any Prince who will only find her and bring her home."

"Who will want to marry a girl he can't see?" said the King. "If they have not married pretty girls they *can* see, they won't care for poor Niente."

"Never mind; we can only try," said the Queen. So she sent out messengers into all the world, and sent the picture of the Princess

(29)

A messenger of the Queen.

everywhere, and proclaimed that the beautiful Princess Niente, and no less than three-quarters of the Kingdom would be given to the Prince that could find the Princess and bring her home. And there was to be a great tournament, or sham fight, at the Palace, to amuse all the Princes before they went on the search. So many Princes gathered together, all full of hope; and they rode against each other with spears and swords, and knocked each other about, and afterwards dined, and danced, and made merry. Some Fairy Knights, too, came over the border, and they fought with spears, riding Beetles and

The Tournament.

Grasshoppers, instead of horses. Here is a picture of a "joust," or tournament, between two sets of Fairy Knights. By all these warlike exercises, they increased their courage till they felt brave enough to fight all the Ghosts, and all the Giants, if only they could save the beautiful Princess.

Well, the tournaments were over, and off all the Princes went into Fairy Land. What funny sights they saw in Fairy Land! They saw a great Snail race, the Snails running so fast, that some of the Fairy jockeys fell off on the grass. They saw a Fairy boy dancing with a

The Great Snail Race.

Dancing with a Squirrel.

Squirrel, and they found all the birds, and all the beasts, quite friendly and kind, and able to talk like other people. This was the way in old times, but now no beasts talk, and no birds, except Parrots only.

Now among all this gallant army of Princes, one was ugly, and he looked old, and odd, and the rest laughed at him, and called him the Prince Comical. But he had a kind heart. One day, when he was out walking alone, and thinking what he could do to find the Princess, he saw three bad boys teasing a big Dragonfly. They had got hold of one of his legs, and were pulling at it with all their might. When the Prince Comical saw this, he ran up and drove the bad boys away, and

What funny sights they saw in Fairy Land!

(32)

rubbed the limb of the Dragonfly, till he gave up groaning and crying. Then the Dragonfly sat up, and said in a weak voice, "You have been very kind to me; what can I do for *you?*"

"Oh, help me," said the Prince, "to find the Princess Niente! *You* fly everywhere; don't you know where she is?"

Cruel Elves.

"*I* don't know," said the Dragonfly, mournfully. "I have never flown so far. But I know that you are all in a very dangerous part of Fairy Land. And I will take you to an aged Black Beetle, who can give you the best advice."

So saying, the Dragonfly walked off with the Prince till they came to the Black Beetle.

"Can *you* tell this Prince," said the Dragonfly, "where the Princess Niente is hidden?"

"I know it is in Mushroom Land," said the Beetle; "but he will want a guide."

"Will *you* be my guide?" asked the Prince.

"Yes," said the Beetle; "but what about your friends, the other Princes?"

"Oh, they must come too; it would not be fair to leave them behind," said the Prince Comical.

He was *the soul of honor;* and though the others laughed at him, he would not take advantage of his luck, and run away from them.

"Well, you *are* a true Knight," said the Black Beetle; "but before we go into the depths of Mushroom Land, just you come here with me."

Then the Black Beetle pointed out to the Prince a great smooth round red thing, a long way off.

"That is the first Mushroom in Mushroom Land," said the Beetle.

Prince Comical spies the sleeping King.

"Now come with me, and you shall see, what you shall see."

So the Prince followed the Beetle, till they came to the Mushroom.

"Climb up and look over," said the Beetle.

So the Prince climbed up, and looked over. There he saw a crowned King, sound asleep.

Here is the Prince Comical (you see he is not very handsome!); and here is the King so sound asleep.

"Try to waken him," said the Beetle; "just try."

So the Prince tried to waken the King, but it was of no use.

"Now, take warning by *that*," said the Black Beetle, "and never go to sleep under a Mushroom in Mushroom country. You will never wake, if you do, till the Princess Niente is found again."

Well, the Prince Comical said he would remember that, and he and the Beetle went off and found the other Princes. They were disposed to laugh at being led by a Black Beetle; but one of them, who was very learned, reminded them that armies had been led before by Wood-peckers, and Wolves, and Humming Birds.

As they marched through Mushroom Land the twilight came upon them, and the Elves began to come out for their dance, for Elves only dance at dusk, and they could not help joining them, which was very imprudent, as they had plenty to do the next day, and it would have

been wiser if they had gone to sleep.

The Elves went on with their play till midnight, and exactly at midnight the Elves stopped their play, and undressed, and got up into the boughs of a big tree and went to sleep. You may wonder how the Elves know when it is midnight, as there are no clocks in Mushroom Land, of course. But they cannot really help knowing, as it is exactly at twelve that the Mushrooms begin to grow, and the little Mushrooms come up.

Wood Elves coming out to dance.

An Elfin dance to greet the night.

The Elves covered every branch of the tree.

Now the Elves covered every branch of the tree, as you see in the picture, and the Princes did not know where to lie down. At last they decided to lie down under a very big Mushroom.

It was in vain that the Black Beetle and Prince Comical warned them to beware.

"Nonsense," they said. *"You* may sleep out in the open air, if you like; we mean to make ourselves comfortable here."

So they all lay down under the shelter of the Mushroom, and Prince Comical slept in the open air. In the morning, he wakened, feeling very well and hungry, and off he set to call his friends. But he might as well have called the Mushroom itself. There they all lay under its shade; and though some of them had their eyes open, not one of them could move. The Prince shook them, dragged them, shouted at them, and pulled their hair. But the more he shouted and dragged, the louder they snored; and the worst of it was, that he could not pull them out of the shadow of the Magic Mushroom. So there he had to leave them, sound asleep.

The Prince thought the Elves could help him perhaps, so he went and asked them how to waken his friends. They were all awake, and the Fairies were dressing the baby-Elves. But they only said, "Oh! it's their fault for sleeping under a Mushroom. Anybody would know that is a stupid thing to do. Besides, we have no time to attend to them, as the sun will be up soon, and we must get these Babies dressed and be off before then."

"Why, where are you going to?" said the Prince.

"Ah! nobody knows where we go to in the day time," said the Elves.

And nobody does.

"Well, what am I to do now?" said the Prince to the Black Beetle.

So there he had to leave them, sound asleep.

"*I* don't know where the Princess is," said the Beetle; "but the Blue Bird is very wise, and *he* may know. Now your best plan will be to steal two of the Blue Bird's eggs, and not give them back till he tells you all he can."

So off they set for the Blue Bird's nest; and, to make a long story short, the Prince stole two of the eggs, and would not give them back, till the Bird promised to tell him all it knew. And the end of it was,

Dressing the Baby Elves.

At first, Prince Comical had a little trouble finding the Blue Bird's nest.

that the Bird carried him to the Court of the Queen of Mushroom Land. She was sitting, in her Crown, on a Mushroom, and she looked very funny and mischievous.

Here you see the Prince, with his hat off, kissing the Queen's hair, and asking for the Princess.

"Oh, *she's* quite safe," said the Queen of Mushroom Land; "but what a funny boy you are. You are not *half* handsome enough for the Princess Niente."

The poor Prince blushed. "They call me Prince Comical," said he; "I know I'm not half good enough!"

"You are *good* enough for anything," said the Queen of Mushroom Land; "but you might be prettier."

Then she touched him with her wand, and he became as handsome a Prince as ever was seen, in a beautiful red silk doublet, slashed with white, and a long gold-colored robe.

Stealing the Blue Bird's eggs.

"*Now* you will do for my Princess Niente," said the Queen of Mushroom Land. "Blue Bird" (and she whispered in the Bird's ear), "take him away to the Princess Niente."

So they flew, and they flew, all day and all night, and next day they

Greeting the Queen of Mushroom Land.

came to a green bower, all full of Fairies, and Butterflies, and funny little people. And there, with all her long yellow hair round her, there sat the Princess Niente. And the Prince Charming laid his Crown at her feet, and knelt on one knee, and asked the Princess to be his love

And the Prince Charming laid his Crown at her feet, and knelt on one knee, and asked the Princess to be his love and his lady.

and his lady. And she did not refuse him, so they were married in the Church of the Elves, and the Glowworm sent his torches, and all the bells of all the flowers made a merry peal. And soon they were to travel home, to the King and the Queen.

CHAPTER THREE

LOST AND FOUND

NOW the Prince had found the Princess, and you might think that they had nothing to do but go home again. The father and mother of the Princess were wearying very much to hear about her. Every day they climbed to the bartizan of the Castle, and looked across the plain, hoping to see dust on the road, and some brave Prince riding back with their daughter. But she never came, and their hair grew gray with sorrow and time. The parents of the other Princes, too, who were all asleep under the Mushroom, were alarmed about their sons, and feared that they had all been taken prisoners, or perhaps eaten up by some Giant. But Princess Niente and Prince Charming were lingering in the enchanted land, too happy to leave the flowers, the brooks, and the Fairies.

The faithful Black Beetle often whispered to the Prince that it was time to turn homewards, but the Prince paid no more attention to his ally than if he had been an Ear-wig. So there, in the Valley Magical, the Prince and Princess might be wandering to this day but for a very sad accident. The night they were married, the Princess had said to the Prince, "Now you may call me Niente, or any pet name you like; but never call me by my own name."

"But I don't know it," said the Prince. "Do tell me what it is?"

"Never," said the Princess; "you must never seek to know it."

"Why not?" said the Prince.

"Something dreadful will happen," said the Princess, "if ever you find out my name, and call me by it."

And she looked quite as if she could be very angry.

Now ever after this, the Prince kept wondering what his wife's real name could be, till he made himself quite unhappy.

"Is it Margaret?" he would say, when he thought the Princess was off her guard; or, "Is it Joan?" "Is it Dorothy?" "It can't be Sybil, can it?"

But she would never tell him.

Poor little Birdie teased.

(50)

Flying away.

Now, one morning, the Princess awoke very early, but she felt so happy that she could not sleep. She lay awake and listened to the Birds singing, and then she watched a Fairy-boy teasing a Bird, which sang (so the boy said) out of tune, and another Fairy-baby riding on a Fly.

At last the Princess, who thought the Prince was sound asleep, began to croon softly a little song she had made about him and her. She had never told him about the song, partly because she was shy, and partly for another reason. So she crooned and hummed to herself,

> *Oh, hand in hand with Gwendoline,*
> *   While yet our locks are gold,*
> *He'll fare among the forests green,*
> *   And through the gardens old;*
> *And when, like leaves that lose their green,*
> *   Our gold has turned to gray,*
> *Then, hand in hand with Gwendoline,*
> *   He'll fade and pass away!*

(51)

"Oh, *Gwendoline* is your name, is it?" said the Prince, who had been wide awake, and listening to her song. And he began to laugh at having found out her secret, and tried to kiss her.

But the Princess turned very, very cold, and white like marble, so that the Prince began to shiver, and he sat down on a fallen Mushroom, and hid his face in his hands, and, in a moment, all his beautiful hair vanished, and his splendid clothes, and his gold train, and his Crown. He wore a red cap, and common clothes, and he was Prince Comical once more. But the Princess arose, and she vanished swiftly away.

Opposite you see the poor Prince crying, and the Princess vanishing away. Thus he was punished for being curious and prying. It is natural, you will say, that a man should like to call his wife by her name. But the Fairies would not allow it, and, what is more, there are still some nations who will not allow a woman to mention the name of her husband.

She runs away, and this is his condition.

Well, here was a sad state of things! The Princess was lost as much as ever, and Prince Charming was changed back into Prince Comical. The Black Beetle sighed day and night, and mingled his tears with those of the Prince. But neither of them knew what to do. They wandered about the Valley Magical, and though it was just as pretty as ever, it seemed quite ugly and stupid to them. The worst of it was, that the Prince felt so foolish. After winning the greatest good fortune, and the dearest bride in the world, he had thrown everything away. He walked about crying, "Oh, Gwen—I mean oh, Niente! dear Niente! return to your own Prince Comical, and all will be forgiven!"

It is impossible to say what would have happened; and probably the Prince would have died of sorrow and hunger (for he ate nothing), if the Black Beetle had not one day met a Bat, which was the favorite charger of Puck. Now Puck, as all the world knows, is the Jester at the Court of Fairy Land. He can make Oberon and Titania—

the King and Queen—laugh at the tricks he plays, and therefore they love him so much that there is nothing they would not do for him. So the Black Beetle began to talk about his master, the Prince, to the Bat Puck commonly rode; and the Bat, a good-natured creature, told the whole story to Puck. Now Puck was also in a good humor, so he jumped at once on his Bat's back, and rode off to consult the King and Queen of Fairy Land. Well, they were sorry for the Prince—he had only broken one little Fairy law after all—and they sent Puck back to tell him what he was to do. This was to find the Blue Bird again, and get the Blue Bird to guide him to the home of the Water Fairy, the Godmother of the Princess.

Long and far the Prince wandered, but at last he found the Blue Bird once more. And the Bird (very good-naturedly) promised to fly in front of him till he led him to the beautiful stream, where the Water Fairy held her court. So they reached it at last, and then the Blue Bird harnessed himself to the chariot of the Water Fairy, and the chariot was the white cup of a Water Lily. Then he pulled, and pulled at the chariot (here he is dragging along the Water Fairy), till he brought her where the Prince was waiting. At first, when she saw him, she was rather angry. "Why did you find out my God-daughter's name?" she said; and the Prince had no excuse to make. He only turned red, and sighed. This rather pleased the Water Fairy.

The Court of the Water Fairy.

"Do you love the Princess very much?" said she.

"Oh, more than all the world," said the Prince.

"Then back you go, to Mushroom Land, and you will find her in the old place. But perhaps she will not be pleased to forgive you at first."

The Prince thought he would chance *that*, but he did not say so. He only bowed very low, and thanked the Water Fairy. Then off he set, with the Blue Bird to guide him, in search of Mushroom Land. At long and at last he reached it, and glad he was to see the little sentinel on the border of the country.

All up and down Mushroom Land the Prince searched, and at last he saw his own Princess, and he rushed up, and knelt at her feet, and held out his hands to ask pardon for having disobeyed the Fairy law.

But she was still rather cross, and down she jumped, and ran round the Mushroom, and he ran after her.

So he chased her for a minute or two, and at last she laughed, and popped up her head over the Mushroom, and pursed up her lips into a cherry. And he kissed her across the Mushroom, and knew he had won back his own dear Princess, and they felt even happier than if they had never been parted.

Puck sitting on a Mushroom.

Asking pardon for his error.

"Journeys end in lovers meeting," and so do Stories. The Prince has his Princess once again, and I can tell you they did not wait long, this time, in the Valley Magical. Off they went, straight home, and the Black Beetle guided them, flying in a bee-line. Just on the farther border of Mushroom Land, they came to all the Princes, fast asleep. But when the Princess drew near, they all wakened, and jumped up, and they slapped the fortunate Prince on the back, and wished him luck, and cried, "Hullo, Comical, old chap; we hardly knew you! Why, you've grown quite handsome!" And so he had; he was changed into Prince Charming again, but he was so happy he never noticed it, for he was not conceited. But the Princess noticed it, and she loved him all the better. Then they all made a procession, with the

A merry chase.

He finds her, and this is the consequence.

A hearty welcome in Fairy Land.

Black Beetle marching at the head; indeed, they called him "Black Rod" now, and he was quite a Courtier.

So with flags flying, and music playing, they returned to the home of the Princess. And the King and Queen met them at the park gates, and fell on the necks of the Prince and Princess, and kissed them, and laughed, and cried for joy, and kissed them again. You may be sure the old Nurse was out among the foremost, her face quite shining with pleasure, and using longer words than the noblest there. And

(59)

she admired the Prince very much, and was delighted that "her girl," as she called the Princess, had got such a good husband. So here we leave them, and that country remained always happy, and so it has neither history nor geography. Therefore you won't find it on any map, nor can you read about it in any book but this book.

Lastly, here is a picture of the Prince and Princess at home, sitting on a beautiful Rose, as a Fairy's God-child can do if she pleases.

As to the Black Beetle, he was appointed to a place about the Court, but he never married, he had no children, and there are no *other* Black Beetles, consequently, in the country where the Prince and Princess became King and Queen.

Home at last.

ERANT OLIM REX QUIDAM ET REGINA
Apuleius.

Au Temps jadis! as Perrault says,
In half-forgotten Fairy days,—
"There lived a King once, and a Queen,
As few there are, as more have been,"—
Ah, still we love the well-worn phrase,
Still love to tread the ancient ways,
To break the fence, to thread the maze,
To see the beauty we have seen,
                    Au Temps jadis!

Here's luck to every child that strays
In Fairy Land among the Fays;
That follows through the forest green
Prince Comical and Gwendoline;
That reads the tales we used to praise,
                    Au Temps jadis!